Get Up, Rick!

F. Isabel Campoy

Illustrated by
Bernard Adnet

Green Light Readers
Harcourt, Inc.

Orlando   Austin   New York
San Diego   Toronto   London

Oh, no! It is late.

Where is Rick?

Is Rick sick?

No! Rick is fast asleep!

Get up, Rick! It is late!

Cock-a-doodle-doo!

Oh, Rick, it is too late.

Now Rick is sad.

We will help Rick.

We will get him a gift.

What is in the sack?

Will it help Rick?

Yes!

Cock-a-doodle-doo!

Response Activity

In this story, the animals talk. What would we hear if we could understand what animals say? Make a page for a class book about what the animals are saying.

- Choose an animal.
- Think about what it might say.
- Draw and write about what your animal says.

It's snack time!

Let's go to the park! Please! Please!

Share your page with your classmates. Put the pages together to make a class book.

Meet the Author
F. Isabel Campoy

F. Isabel Campoy lives on a ranch part of the year. A rooster wakes her up every morning. "He doesn't have an alarm clock, either!" she says. "I wanted to imagine the opposite situation, and so I wrote about Rick."

Meet the Illustrator
Bernard Adnet

Bernard Adnet grew up in France. As a child, he spent many hours alone drawing, but he also drew for his nieces and nephews. Today, he still makes children happy with his drawings.

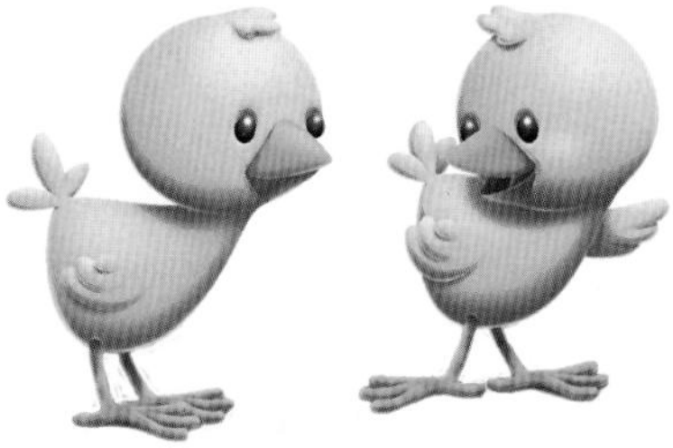

Green Light Readers
For the reader who's ready to GO!

"A must-have for any family with a beginning reader."—*Boston Sunday Herald*

"You can't go wrong with adding several copies of these terrific books to your beginning-to-read collection."—*School Library Journal*

"A winner for the beginner."—*Booklist*

Five Tips to Help Your Child Become a Great Reader

1. Get involved. Reading aloud to and with your child is just as important as encouraging your child to read independently.

2. Be curious. Ask questions about what your child is reading.

3. Make reading fun. Allow your child to pick books on subjects that interest her or him.

4. Words are everywhere—not just in books. Practice reading signs, packages, and cereal boxes with your child.

5. Set a good example. Make sure your child sees YOU reading.

Why Green Light Readers Is the Best Series for Your New Reader

• Created exclusively for beginning readers by some of the biggest and brightest names in children's books

• Reinforces the reading skills your child is learning in school

• Encourages children to read—and finish—books by themselves

• Offers extra enrichment through fun, age-appropriate activities unique to each story

• Incorporates characteristics of the Reading Recovery program used by educators

• Developed with Harcourt School Publishers and credentialed educational consultants

www.HarcourtBooks.com

First Green Light Readers edition 2007

Green Light Readers is a trademark of Harcourt, Inc., registered in the United States of America and/or other jurisdictions.

Library of Congress Cataloging-in-Publication Data
Campoy, F. Isabel.
Get up, Rick!/F. Isabel Campoy; illustrated by Bernard Adnet.
p. cm.
"Green Light Readers."
Summary: When Rick the rooster sleeps through the sunrise, his clever friends give him just the thing to help.
[1. Roosters—Fiction.] I. Adnet, Bernard, ill. II. Title.
PZ7.C16153Ge 2007
[E]—dc22   2006035418
ISBN 978-0-15-206266-8
ISBN 978-0-15-206272-9 (pb)

A C E G H F D B
A C E G H F D B (pb)

Ages 4-6
Grade: I
Guided Reading Level: C
Reading Recovery Level: 4